williambee

Stanley
the Builder

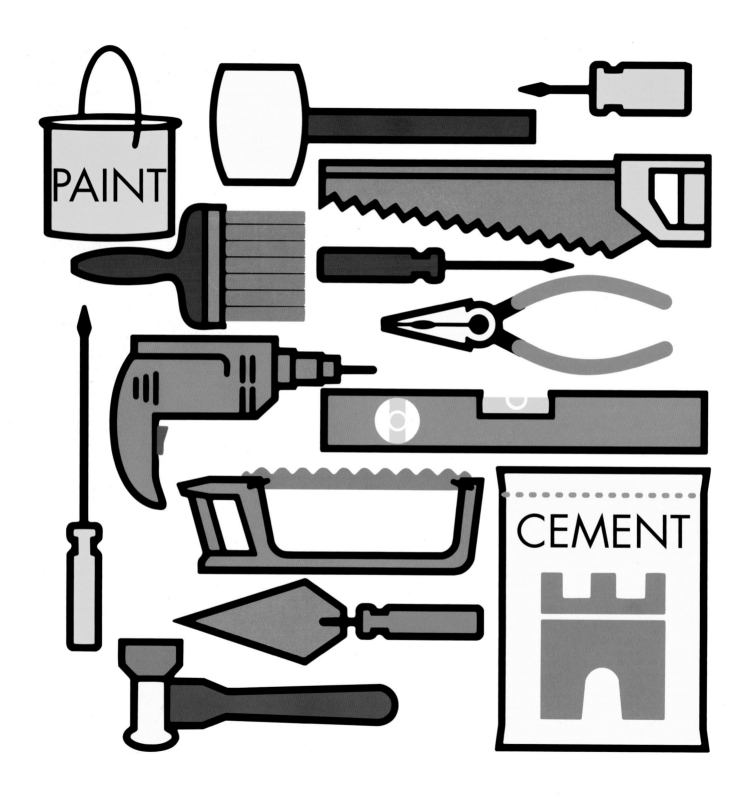

Published by
PEACHTREE PUBLISHERS
1700 Chattahoochee Avenue
Atlanta, Georgia 30318-2112
www.peachtree-online.com

Text and illustrations © 2014 by William Bee

First published in Great Britain in 2014 by Jonathan Cape,
an imprint of Random House Children's Publishers UK
First United States version published in 2014 by Peachtree Publishers
First paperback edition published in 2014 by Peachtree Publishers

The illustrations were rendered digitally

Printed and bound in May 2016 by Leo Paper Products in China

10 9 8 7 6 5 4 3 2 (hardcover)
10 9 8 7 6 5 4 3 2 (paperback)

Library of Congress Cataloging-in-Publication Data

Bee, William, author, illustrator.
Stanley the builder / by William Bee.
pages cm
ISBN: 978-1-56145-801-1 (hardcover)
ISBN 978-1-56145-822-6 (trade paperback)
Summary: "What a job for Stanley—he's building a house for his friend, Myrtle.
He will need his digger and his bulldozer and his cement mixer. He will also need his friend,
Charlie to help. But will they manage to build the whole house?"— Provided by publisher.
[1. Building—Fiction. 2. Dwellings—Fiction. 3. Hamsters—Fiction. 4. Rodents—Ficton.] I. Title.
PZ7.B38197St 2014
[E]—dc23
2013049352

williambee
Stanley
the Builder

Ω
PEACHTREE
ATLANTA

What are Stanley and Myrtle doing?

Myrtle has just bought a plot of land.
She asks Stanley to build her
a new house.

First Stanley clears the site with his orange bulldozer.

Then he digs out the foundations with his yellow digger.

Charlie has come to help.

Stanley pours the cement into the hole.
Don't walk on it! It's still wet!

Laying bricks is very tricky work.
Stanley taps the bricks down.
Charlie checks that they are level.

Stanley uses his green crane to lift the beams up onto the roof.

Building houses is hot work!
Myrtle has brought Stanley and Charlie
some orange juice. Thank you, Myrtle!

Charlie nails the shingles onto the roof.
Stanley puts the windows into
the holes in the walls.

Finally Stanley and Charlie paint the house in Myrtle's favorite colors . . .

Red, white, and blue!

Myrtle is very pleased with her new house.
It's beautiful! Thank you, Stanley!
Thank you, Charlie!

Well! What a busy day!

Time for supper!
Time for a bath!

And time for bed!
Goodnight, Stanley.

Stanley

If you liked **Stanley the Builder** then you'll love these other books about Stanley:

Stanley's Diner
Stanley the Farmer
Stanley's Garage

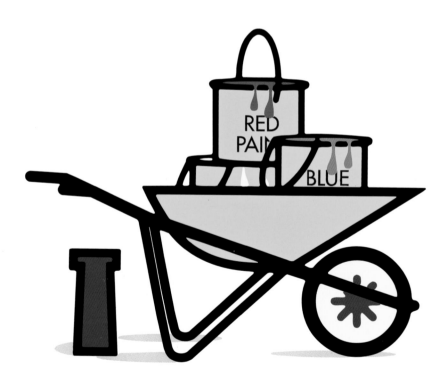